Segue Institute for Learning
"Where ALL Students are At Promise"
325 Cowden Street
Central Falls, RI 02863

Copyright © 2001 by Michael Neugebauer Verlag,
an imprint of Nord–Süd Verlag AG, Gossau Zürich, Switzerland
First published in Switzerland under the title WIE DAS KAMEL ZU SEINEM HÖCKER KAM

First published in the United States, Great Britain, Canada,
Australia, and New Zealand in 2001 by North–South Books,
an imprint of Nord–Süd Verlag AG, Gossau Zürich, Switzerland.
First paperback edition published in 2003 by North–South Books.

Distributed in the United States by North–South Books Inc., New York.

Library of Congress Cataloging-in-Publication Data
Kipling, Rudyard, 1865–1936.
How the camel got his hump / Rudyard Kipling; illustrated by Lisbeth Zwerger.
p.   cm.
"A Michael Neugebauer book."
Summary: Relates how the camel received his permanent hump from the Djinn of All Deserts.
[1. Camels—Fiction.] I. Zwerger, Lisbeth, ill. II. Title.
PZ7.K632 Hf 2001   [E]—dc21   2001034559

A CIP catalogue record for this book is available from The British Library.
ISBN 0-7358-1482-1 (trade edition) 10 9 8 7 6 5 4 3 2 1
ISBN 0-7358-1483-X (library edition) 10 9 8 7 6 5 4 3 2 1
ISBN 0-7358-1870-3 (paperback edition) 10 9 8 7 6 5 4 3 2 1
Printed in Italy

For more information about our books, and the authors and artists
who create them, visit our web site: www.northsouth.com

Rudyard Kipling

HOW THE CAMEL GOT HIS HUMP

Illustrated by Lisbeth Zwerger

A Michael Neugebauer Book
North–South Books / New York / London

Now this tale tells how the Camel got his big hump.

In the beginning of years, when the world was so new-and-all, and the Animals were just beginning to work for Man, there was a Camel, and he lived in the middle of a Howling Desert because he did not want to work; and besides, he was a Howler himself. So he ate sticks and thorns and tamarisks and milkweed and prickles, most 'scruciating idle; and when anybody spoke to him he said 'Humph!' Just 'Humph!' and no more.

Presently the Horse came to him on Monday morning, with a saddle on his back and a bit in his mouth, and said, 'Camel, O Camel, come out and trot like the rest of us.'

'Humph!' said the Camel; and the Horse went away and told the Man.
 Presently the Dog came to him, with a stick in his mouth, and said,
'Camel, O Camel, come and fetch and carry like the rest of us.'
'Humph!' said the Camel; and the Dog went away and told the Man.
 Presently the Ox came to him, with the yoke on his neck, and said,
'Camel, O Camel, come and plough like the rest of us.'
'Humph!' said the Camel; and the Ox went away and told the Man.

At the end of the day the Man called the Horse and the Dog and the Ox together, and said, 'Three, O Three, I'm very sorry for you (with the world so new-and-all); but that Humph-thing in the Desert can't work, or he would have been here by now, so I am going to leave him alone, and you must work double-time to make up for it.'

That made the Three very angry (with the world so new-and-all), and they held a palaver, and an *indaba*, and a *punchayet*, and a pow-wow on the edge of the Desert; and the Camel came chewing milkweed *most* 'scruciating idle, and laughed at them. Then he said 'Humph!' and went away again.

Presently there came along the Djinn in charge of All Deserts, rolling in a cloud of dust (Djinns always travel that way because it is Magic), and he stopped to palaver and pow-wow with the Three.

'Djinn of All Deserts,' said the Horse, '*is* it right for any one to be idle, with the world so new-and-all?'

'Certainly not,' said the Djinn.

'Well,' said the Horse, 'there's a thing in the middle of your Howling Desert (and he's a Howler himself) with a long neck and long legs, and he hasn't done a stroke of work since Monday morning. He won't trot.'

'Whew!' said the Djinn, whistling, 'that's my Camel, for all the gold in Arabia! What does he say about it?'

'He says "Humph!"' said the Dog; 'and he won't fetch and carry.'

'Does he say anything else?'

'Only "Humph!"; and he won't plough,' said the Ox.

'Very good,' said the Djinn. 'I'll humph him if you will kindly wait a minute.'

The Djinn rolled himself up in his dustcloak, and took a bearing across the Desert, and found the Camel most 'scruciatingly idle, looking at his own reflection in a pool of water.

'My long and bubbling friend,' said the Djinn, 'what's this I hear of your doing no work, with the world so new-and-all?'

'Humph!' said the Camel.

The Djinn sat down, with his chin in his hand, and began to think a Great Magic, while the Camel looked at his own reflection in the pool of water.

'You've given the Three extra work ever since Monday morning, all on account of your 'scruciating idleness,' said the Djinn; and he went on thinking Magics, with his chin in his hand.

'Humph!' said the Camel.

'I shouldn't say that again if I were you,' said the Djinn; 'you might say it once too often. Bubbles, I want you to work.'

And the Camel said 'Humph!' again; but no sooner had he said it than he saw his back, that he was so proud of, puffing up and puffing up into a great big lolloping humph.

This is the picture of the Djinn making the beginnings of the Magic that brought the Humph to the Camel. First he drew a line in the air with his finger, and it became solid; and then he made a cloud, and then he made an egg—you can see them at the bottom of the picture—and then there was a magic pumpkin that turned into a big white flame. Then the Djinn took his magic fan and fanned that flame till the flame turned into a Magic by itself. It was a good Magic and a very kind Magic really, though it had to give the Camel a Humph because the Camel was lazy. The Djinn in charge of All Deserts was one of the nicest of the Djinns, so he would never do anything really unkind.

Here is the picture of the Djinn in charge of All Deserts guiding the Magic with his magic fan. The Camel is eating a twig of acacia, and he has just finished saying 'humph' once too often (the Djinn told him he would), and so the Humph is coming. The long towelly-thing growing out of the thing like an onion is the Magic, and you can see the Humph on its shoulder. The Humph fits on the flat part of the Camel's back. The Camel is too busy looking at his own beautiful self in the pool of water to know what is going to happen to him.

Underneath the truly picture is a picture of the world so new-and-all. There are two smoky volcanoes in it, some other mountains and some stones and a lake and a black island and a twisty river and a lot of other things, as well as a Noah's Ark. I couldn't draw all the deserts that the Djinn was in charge of, so I only drew one, but it is a most deserty desert.

'Do you see that?' said the Djinn. 'That's your very own humph that you've brought upon your very own self by not working. Today is Thursday, and you've done no work since Monday, when the work began. Now you are going to work.'

'How can I,' said the Camel, 'with this humph on my back?'

'That's made a-purpose,' said the Djinn, 'all because you missed those three days. You will be able to work now for three days without eating, because you can live on your humph; and don't you ever say I never did anything for you. Come out of the Desert and go to the Three, and behave. Humph yourself!'

And the Camel humphed himself, humph and all, and went away to join the Three. And from that day to this the Camel always wears a humph (we call it 'hump' now, not to hurt his feelings); but he has never yet caught up with the three days that he missed at the beginning of the world, and he has never yet learned how to behave.

Segue Institute for Learning
"Where ALL Students are At Promise"
325 Cowden Street
Central Falls, RI 02863